MW01155409

LAURA CARLIN

LONDON

A HISTORY

CANDLEWICK STUDIO

an imprint of Candlewick Press

When you have entered England, if you should come to London, you will quickly pass through it, as that city greatly displeases me. . . . No one lives in it without offence; there is not a single street in it, that does not abound in miserable obscene wretches; there, in proportion as any man has exceeded in wickedness, so much is he the better. . . . Behold, I warn you, whatever of evil or of perversity there is in any, whatever in all parts of the world, you will find in that city alone. Go not to the dances of panders, nor mix yourself up with the herds of the stews; avoid the talus and the dice, the theatre and the tavern. You will find more braggadocios there than in all France, while the number of flatterers is infinite. Stage players, buffoons, those that have no hair on their bodies, Garamantes [*sic*], pickthanks . . . lewd musical girls, druggists, lustful persons, fortune-tellers, extortioners, nightly strollers, magicians, mimics, common beggars, tatterdemalions,—this whole crew has filled every house. So if you do not wish to live with the shameful, you will not dwell in London.

Richard of Devizes, The Chronicle of Richard of Devizes, *1192*

CONTENTS

*SEE EXTRA NOTES

In some cases, a date is representative of a particular time period
over which an event or movement occurred.

2.6 MILLION—11,700 YEARS AGO, THE PLEISTOCENE EPOCH

The island of Britain started separating from the mainland 450,000 years ago. Ice sheets formed and melted, causing the river Thames to rise and recede. Temperatures could fluctuate between warm, balmy conditions and long periods of cold and ice.

9700 BCE, THE STONE AGE

Early creatures living in Britain included woolly mammoths, cave lions, and hippos. The earliest evidence of humans in the London area dates to the Paleolithic Period. These early people's nomadic life involved constant travel in family groups as they hunted or foraged for food.

700 BCE, THE IRON AGE

Over time, the Thames began to follow a more
familiar course. Tribes living near the river created
new open spaces along its banks for hunting, growing
plants, and rearing animals. They cultivated the
land with stronger tools made of iron. They built
hill forts and lived more settled lives.

The last *Age* was of hard iron. Immediately every
species of crime burst forth, in this age of degenerated
tendencies; modesty, truth and honor took flight; in their
place succeeded fraud, deceit, treachery, violence, and the
cursed hankering for acquisition.

Ovid, "The Iron Age," Metamorphoses, 8 CE

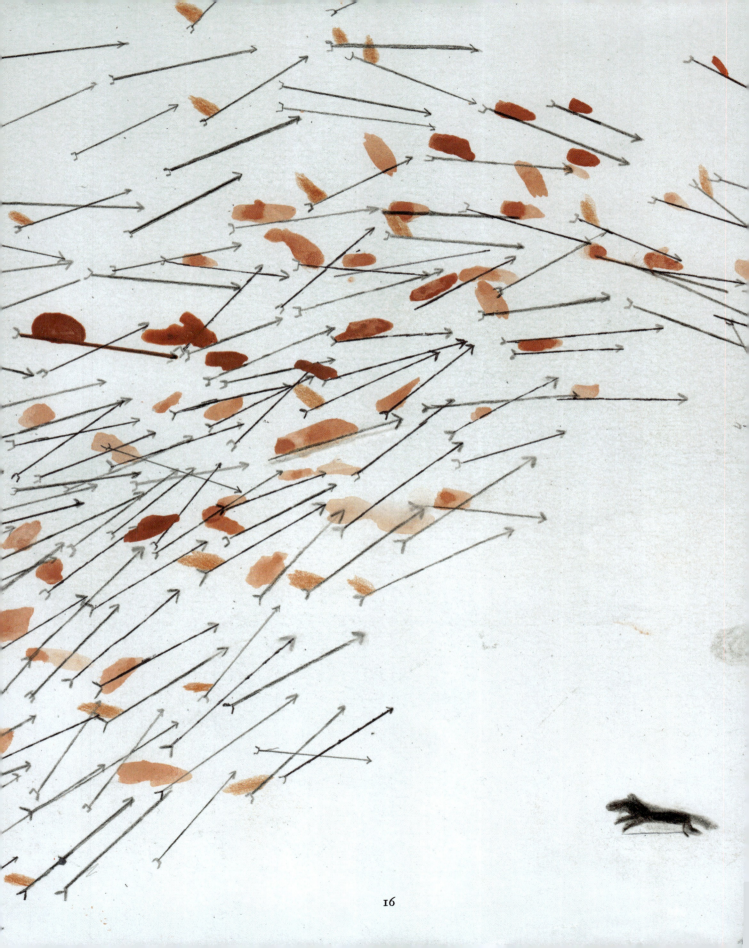

43 CE, THE ROMANS ATTACK

In order to legitimize his rule to the senators and people of Rome, the emperor Claudius mounted an invasion of Britannia. He was determined to succeed where even the great Julius Caesar had failed: in conquering this mysterious island at the edge of the Roman world.

The Roman army reportedly brought huge war elephants with them across the English Channel. They would have been a fearsome sight, along with the Roman soldiers who were famed for their battle prowess. The soldiers were reputed to have swum across rivers, including the Thames, in full armor.

Thence the Britons retired to the river Thames at a point near where it empties into the ocean and the latter's flood-tide forms a lake. This they crossed easily because they knew where the firm ground in this locality and the easy passages were; but the Romans in following them up came to grief at this spot . . . [and] lost many men.

Dio Cassius, Monumenta Historica Britannica, *211 CE–233 CE*

53 CE, A BRIDGE INTO LONDINIUM

Claudius's invasion of Britain helped establish London, or Londinium, as a thriving, cosmopolitan merchant town. His men built a bridge across the Thames and put up a fort to guard the town.

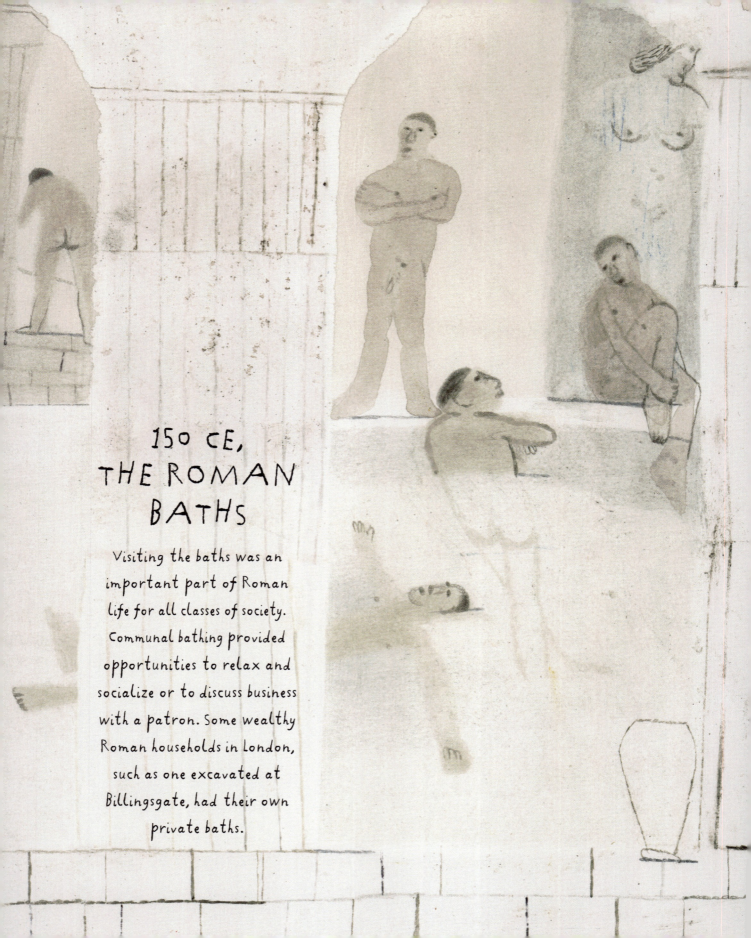

150 CE, THE ROMAN BATHS

Visiting the baths was an important part of Roman life for all classes of society. Communal bathing provided opportunities to relax and socialize or to discuss business with a patron. Some wealthy Roman households in London, such as one excavated at Billingsgate, had their own private baths.

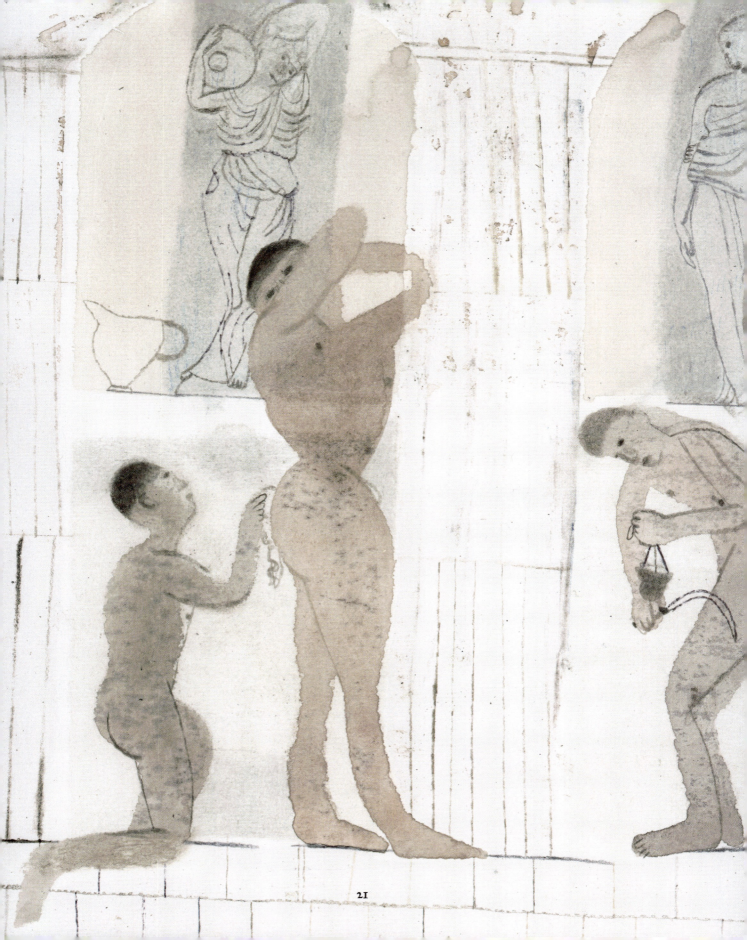

200 CE, THE ROMAN AMPHITHEATER

The Roman amphitheater in Guildhall Yard could seat around 7,000 spectators. London's estimated population at the time was around 25,000.

The events held here were of a bloodthirsty variety. Fighting against animals took place in the morning, with gladiator fights in the late afternoon. Public executions were around midday.

For so soon as he saw that blood, he therewith drunk down savageness; nor turned away, but fixed his eye, drinking in frenzy, unawares, and was delighted with that guilty fight, and intoxicated with the bloody pastime.

Saint Augustine, Confessions, *c. 400 CE*

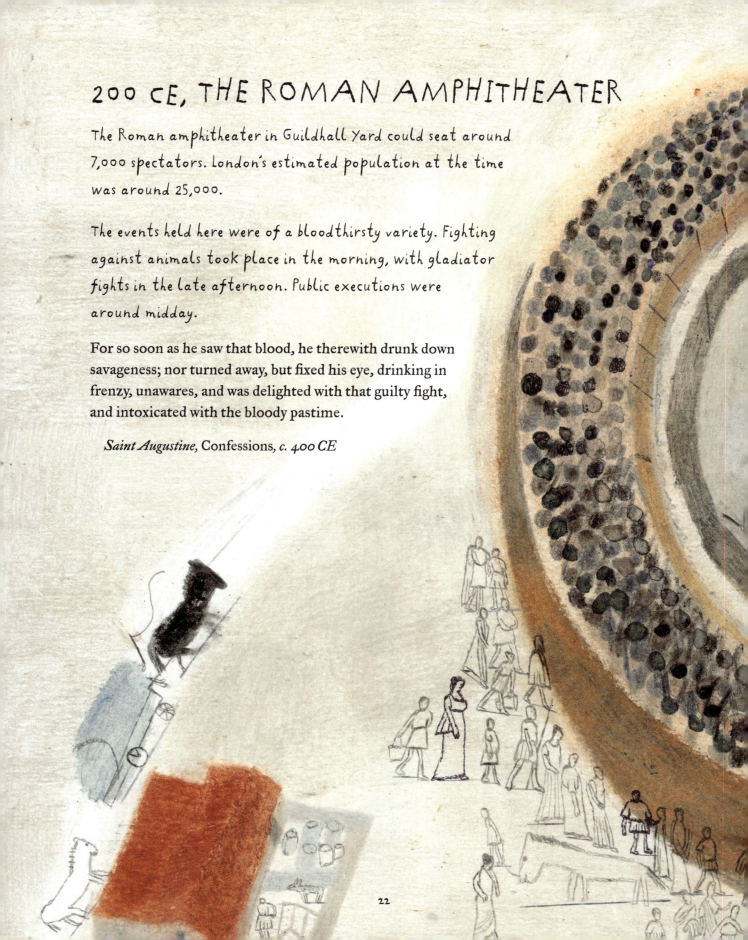

409 CE, LONDINIUM ABANDONED

After more than 350 years of occupation, the Romans withdrew suddenly from Britain and deserted Londinium.

[Emperor] Honorius, having sent letters to the cities of Britain, counsel[ed] them to be watchful of their own security.

Zosimus, New History, *early sixth century CE*

410 CE–1066 CE, THE ANGLO-SAXONS

The early Anglo-Saxon settlers founded their own town of Lundenwic outside the abandoned Londinium, in the area that would become Covent Garden. They named the walled ruins of the Roman city Lundenburh. Lundenwic was a messy trading town interspersed with confusing, muddy paths, very different from the Roman city of Londinium.

793 CE, THE VIKINGS

London suffered many attacks by the fearsome warriors known as Vikings who came across the seas from Scandinavia.

The same year came three hundred and fifty ships into the mouth of the Thames; the crew of which went upon land, and stormed Canterbury and London; putting to flight Bertulf, king of the Mercians, with his army; and then marched southward over the Thames into Surrey. Here Ethelwulf and his son Ethelbald, at the head of the West-Saxon army, fought with them at Ockley, and made the greatest slaughter of the heathen army that we have ever heard reported to this present day. There also they [the West-Saxons] obtained the victory.

Anonymous, The Anglo-Saxon Chronicle, *851 CE*

886 CE, ALFRED REBUILDS LONDON

King Alfred the Great reestablished English control of London and restored its defenses. The old Roman walls were repaired, inhabitants were moved from Lundenwic to Lundenburh, and the old Roman city became a center of population once more.

After the burning of cities and massacres of the people, [Alfred] honorably rebuilt the city of London [and] made it habitable.

Bishop Asser, Life of Alfred, *893 CE*

900 CE–1012 CE, VIKING ATTACKS

London continued to be attacked and periodically captured by Viking raiders.

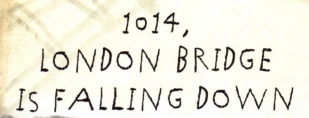

1014,
LONDON BRIDGE
IS FALLING DOWN

After the death of Alfred the Great, Danish Vikings recaptured and occupied London. In 1014, a combined force of Anglo-Saxons and Norwegian Vikings sailed up the Thames to reclaim the conquered city. The Danes, from their vantage point of London Bridge, hurled spears at their enemies. However, the attackers pulled the roofs off nearby houses and held them over their heads in the boats, enabling them to get near enough to the bridge to attach ropes to its supports and bring London Bridge down.

London Bridge is falling down,
Falling down, falling down,
London Bridge is falling down,
My fair lady.

Anonymous, English nursery rhyme,
early seventeenth century

1066, THE MIDDLE AGES: HALLEY'S COMET

Many people thought that the appearance of Halley's comet in 1066 was a warning of terrible things to come . . .

"Thou art come! a matter of lamentation to many a mother art thou
come; I have seen thee long since; but I now behold thee much more
terrible, threatening to hurl destruction on this country."

William of Malmesbury, quoting Eilmer of Malmesbury,
Deeds of English Kings, *1125*

1066, THE NORMANS: WILLIAM CROWNED KING*

Having won the Battle of Hastings on October 14, 1066, the Norman king William, known as William the Conqueror, took a little longer to capture London. He was crowned king of England at Westminster Abbey on Christmas Day 1066.

1070, NORMAN TOWN

Under the protection of the Norman empire, London's overseas trade grew and new docks were built along the riverbank. The city became a hub of different cultures, with Norman, French, German, Norwegian, Danish, and Flemish inhabitants. Most houses were small and wooden with thatched roofs, often with living quarters located above a shop.

c. 1100, STREET NAMES OF LONDON*

Many London street names date to the twelfth and thirteenth centuries. Different districts reflected the traders who worked there. A number of streets in present-day London, such as Milk Street, Cinnamon Street, Honey Lane, and Poultry, still hark back to those businesses.

SEETHING LANE

THIS IS THE CORNER OF FLEET STREET 1660

CITY OF ✚ LONDON
BEAR GARDENS
S.E.1

KNIGHTRIDER ST

CITY OF LONDON

UPPER
BUTTS

←

SOHO STREET
1600

DOWNING
STREET SW1
CITY OF WESTMINSTER

WARDROBE
PLACE

FETTER LANE

SHOOTERS
HILL

BIRD
- CAGE -
WALK

43

1215, MAGNA CARTA AND THE FIRST PARLIAMENT*

In 1215, King John was forced to sign Magna Carta, the first bill of rights, which limited the power of the English sovereign and gave proper rights to the people, including the principle of habeas corpus, which mandated that no one could be imprisoned unlawfully. It allowed for the development of Parliament as we understand it today and was the first step toward establishing a free and open democracy.

No freeman may be apprehended, or imprisoned, or disseised of his freehold, or liberties, or free customs, or be outlawed or banished, or any wise destroyed. Nor will we pass upon him, nor condemn him, but by the lawful judgment of his peers, or by the law of the land.

Magna Carta, 1215

1235, HENRY III STARTS A ROYAL MENAGERIE*

Medieval monarchs were often presented with rare and unusual animals by other rulers. Henry III received lions, leopards, and even an African elephant. Refusing and returning them would have been insulting, so Henry used the animals to create the first zoo at the Tower of London. One resident was a polar bear, a gift from the king of Norway. With a chain around its neck, the bear was allowed to catch fish in the Thames.

1348, THE BLACK DEATH

The bubonic plague, known as the Black Death, arrived in England in 1348 with devastating effect. It is estimated that around half of London's population died in two years.

Physicians advised on cures for the terrible disease, which were supplied by apothecaries, while surgeries were carried out by barbers. Very few of these measures were effective. Remedies included rubbing raw onion or a live chicken on the inflamed lymph nodes caused by the illness. Another purported cure was to show repentance, sometimes through enduring pain, as it was believed that the illness was a punishment from God. Provision for the sick and poor was the responsibility of parish churches, but from the twelfth century monasteries began to form hospitals, such as Saint Thomas's and Saint Bartholomew's.

In 1349 over six hundred men came to London from Flanders. . . . Each wore a cap marked with a red cross in front and behind. Each had in his right hand a scourge with three nails. Each tail had a knot and through the middle of it there were sometimes sharp nails fixed. They marched naked in a file one behind the other and whipped themselves with these scourges on their naked bleeding bodies.

Robert of Avesbury, Historia de Mirabilibus Gestis Eduardi III, *1720*

1381,
THE PEASANTS'
REVOLT

Angered by high taxes, a contingent of rebels from Kent, in southeastern England, marched on London in 1381. Despite little being known about their leader, Wat Tyler, the revolt is known as Wat Tyler's Rebellion.

52

On June 15, fourteen-year-old King Richard left the city to meet Tyler and the rebels at Smithfield. While Richard and Tyler were talking, the Lord Mayor of London stabbed Tyler.

With Tyler dead, Richard was able to persuade the rebels to return home, promising to meet many of their demands. In fact, Richard promptly rescinded his promises and did nothing to help them.

Tyler said to the mayor: "A [*sic*] God's name what have I said to displease thee?" "Yes, truly," quoth the mayor, "thou false stinking knave, shalt thou speak thus in the presence of the king my natural lord? I commit never to live, without thou shalt dearly abye it." And with those words the mayor drew out his sword and strake Tyler so great a stroke on the head, that he fell down at the feet of his horse, and as soon as he was fallen, they environed him all about, whereby he was not seen of his company. Then a squire of the king's alighted, called John Standish, and he drew out his sword and put it into Wat Tyler's belly, and so he died.

Jean Froissart, Chronicles, *1400*

1390, THE SMITHFIELD TOURNAMENT

As a large, open space close to the city, Smithfield was for centuries the main site for the public execution of heretics and dissidents in London. It was also used for tournaments, extravagant spectacles in which knights and nobles could publicly demonstrate their skills. Tournaments attracted huge crowds, including women, and flaunted idealized images of knighthood and chivalry.

The king of England ordered grand tournaments and feasts to be holden in the city of London, where sixty knights should be accompanied by sixty noble ladies, richly ornamented and dressed. The sixty knights were to tilt for two days; that is to say, on the Sunday after Michaelmas-day, and the Monday following in the year of grace 1390. The sixty knights were to set out at two o'clock in the afternoon from the Tower of London, with their ladies, and parade through the streets, down Cheapside, to a large square called Smithfield. There the knights were to wait on the Sunday the arrival of any foreign knights who might be desirous of tilting; and this feast of the Sunday was called the challengers.

The same ceremonies were to take place on the Monday, and the sixty knights to be prepared for tilting courteously with blunted lances against all comers. The prize for the best knight of the opponents was to be a rich crown of gold, that for the tenants of the lists a very rich golden clasp: they were to be given to the most gallant tilter, according to the judgment of the ladies, who would be present with the queen of England and the great barons, as spectators. . . .

. . . In this procession they moved on through the streets of London, attended by numbers of minstrels and trumpets, to Smithfield. The queen of England and her ladies and damsels were already arrived and placed in chambers handsomely decorated. . . .

The tournament now began, and every one exerted himself to the utmost to excel: many were unhorsed, and more lost their helmets. The j[o]usting continued with great courage and perseverance until night put an end to it. The company now retired to their lodgings or their homes; and, when the hour for supper was near, the lords and ladies attended it, which was splendid and well served.

Jean Froissart, Chronicles, *1400*

But Brain gazed straight ahead his lance
To aim more faithfully.
They charged, they struck; both fell, both bled.
Brain rose again, ungloved,
Heart, dying, smiled and faintly said,
"My love to my beloved!"

*Sidney Lanier, "The Tournament:
Joust First," 1899*

1476, THE CANTERBURY TALES

The Canterbury Tales, written by Geoffrey Chaucer, were very popular in medieval England. Chaucer structures the tales as part of a story-telling contest among a group of pilgrims traveling together from London to Canterbury to visit the shrine of Saint Thomas Becket. The prize is a free meal at the Tabard Inn in Southwark on their return, yet it is never revealed who won as Chaucer didn't finish the tales.

Bifel that, in that seson on a day,
In Southwerk at the Tabard as I lay
Redy to wenden on my pilgrimage
To Caunterbury with ful devout corage,
At night was come in-to that hostelrye
Wel nyne and twenty in a companye,
Of sondry folk, by aventure y-falle
In felawshipe, and pilgrims were they alle,
That toward Caunterbury wolden ryde;
The chambres and the stables weren wyde,
And wel we weren esed atte beste.
And shortly, whan the sonne was to reste,
So hadde I spoken with hem everichon,
That I was of hir felawshipe anon,
And made forward erly for to ryse,
To take our wey, ther as I yow devyse.

Geoffrey Chaucer, The Canterbury Tales, *1476*

1500, LONDON GROWS

With a population of about 60,000 and open fields near the city, London was far from the sprawling metropolis it is today.

CATHERINE OF ARAGON   ANNE BOLEYN   JANE SEYMOUR   ANNE OF CLEVES   CATHERINE HOWARD   CATHERI PAR

1509, HENRY VIII

Henry VIII was one of England's most memorable monarchs. During his thirty-seven-year reign, which began in 1509, Henry married six wives and made radical changes to the country, including vastly expanding the Royal Navy and breaking with the Catholic Church.

The King, famous for his extravagant tastes, turned Hampton Court into a spectacular pleasure palace, the most impressive in England. It became Henry's favorite residence, visited by all six of his wives. Some were even given apartments there. The King was particularly demanding about his own living quarters, having them rebuilt several times.

His Majesty . . . is the handsomest potentate I ever set eyes on; above the usual height, with an extremely fine calf to his leg, his complexion very fair and bright, with auburn hair combed straight and short in the French fashion . . . his throat being rather long and thick.

Pasqualigo, a Venetian diplomat, in a dispatch back to Venice, 1515

OVERLEAF

1530s, HYDE PARK

One of the oldest royal parks in London, Hyde Park used to belong to the Church of England as part of Westminster Abbey. In 1536, King Henry VIII took large sections in order to create his own hunting grounds ranging from Whitehall Palace to Kensington village. The parcel is now known as Hyde Park and Kensington Gardens.

1533, THE THAMES

For Londoners, travel via the river proved the most convenient and enjoyable form of transportation. Henry VIII often traveled by barge between London and Hampton Court Palace. The very wealthiest built their palaces facing the river, giving them direct access to their boats.

Throughout London's history, kings and queens have used the river for ceremonial celebrations, processions, and funerals. For Anne Boleyn's coronation, Henry VIII ordered a magnificent river procession to the

Tower of London. It was made up of over 300 boats and barges—one bearing mechanical monsters and a fire-breathing dragon.

Just three years later, Anne was to take the same journey to the Tower, but this time to her imprisonment and eventual execution.

"I am come hither to die; for according to the law, and by the law I am judged to die; and therefore I will speak nothing against it. . . . I pray God save the king . . . for a gentler nor a more merciful prince was there never."

Edward Hall, reporting Anne Boleyn's last words, Hall's Chronicle, *1548*

1553, BLOODY MARY

In 1553, Mary I successfully forestalled an attempt to install Jane Grey on the throne and became the first woman to be crowned a ruling queen of England.

Mary was on the throne for only five years, a reign in which she zealously tried to restore Roman Catholicism in England. The brutality of her methods earned her the nickname "Bloody Mary." She had around 280 Protestants burned at the stake as heretics for refusing to convert to Catholicism, and a further 800 fled into exile.

As known to your Serenity, England is now ruled by Queen Mary and by her husband, Philip of Austria, King of Spain. To commence with her, as mistress of the kingdom, she was born (of Henry VIII. and Katharine of Aragon, daughter of King Ferdinand the Catholic, his first and legitimate wife) in the month of February 1516.... Few other women in the world of her rank ever lived more wretchedly ... for with very great indignity she had to serve as her mistress (*come a patrona*) a public strumpet (*una publica meretrice*), her father's concubine, that famous Anne Boleyn, whom she saw not only succeed to her mother's place, but also, during that mother's lifetime, raised to the crown of England.

Calendar of State Papers Relating to English Affairs
in the Archives of Venice, *1555–1558, 1877*

1559, ELIZABETH I*

After the death of her half sister, Queen Mary, Elizabeth I ascended the throne at the age of twenty-five. Her coronation took place on January 15, 1559, at Westminster Abbey. It was the last coronation in Great Britain to be conducted under the authority of the Catholic Church.

Her face oblong, fair, but wrinkled; her eyes small, yet black and pleasant; her nose a little hooked; her lips narrow, and her teeth black (a defect the English seem subject to, from their too great use of sugar) . . . she wore false hair, and that red; upon her head she had a small crown . . . her bosom was uncovered, as all the English ladies have it till they marry . . . her hands were small, her fingers long, and her stature neither tall nor low; her air was stately, her manner of speaking mild and obliging.

Paul Hentzner, Travels in England During the Reign of Queen Elizabeth, *1892*

1559, THE COPPERPLATE MAP

The earliest true bird's-eye view map of London.

"Soon London will be all England."

James I, early seventeenth century

1599, THE GLOBE THEATRE*

The original Globe Theatre was built by the Lord Chamberlain's Men,
the company in which William Shakespeare was an actor,
playwright-in-residence, and part owner. It is thought
that *Julius Caesar* was the first Shakespeare play
performed at the original Globe.

All the world's a stage,
And all the men and women merely players;
They have their exits and their entrances;
And one man in his time plays many parts,
His acts being seven ages.

William Shakespeare,
As You Like It, *1623*

c. 1570–c. 1846, DELFTWARE

Immigrants from Flanders, fleeing religious persecution, settled in England and introduced their tin-glazed earthenware to England. Potteries specializing in delftware flourished in London, especially around Southwark and Lambeth. The name comes from the town of Delft in the Netherlands.

OVERLEAF

c. 1550s–c. 1650, FILTHY LONDON

Between the mid-sixteenth and mid-seventeenth centuries, the population of London rose rapidly, increasing from 80,000 to over 300,000. For many, it was a dirty, smelly, and unsanitary place with a high death rate.

79

1605, THE GUNPOWDER PLOT

The Gunpowder Plot was a failed attempt to assassinate King James I of England. A group of devout Roman Catholics, led by Robert Catesby, orchestrated the plan to return England to Catholic rule by blowing up the Protestant king, his queen, and his heir at the Opening of Parliament.

In the early hours of November 5, 1605, royal guards discovered Guy Fawkes, one of the conspirators, in the cellar directly beneath the House of Lords. He was carrying fuses and matches. Thirty-six barrels of gunpowder were later discovered. Fawkes and his accomplices were found guilty of treason and put to death.

1606, FIREWORKS NIGHT*

Remember, remember!
The fifth of November,
The Gunpowder treason and plot;
I know of no reason
Why the Gunpowder treason
Should ever be forgot!
Guy Fawkes and his companions
Did the scheme contrive,
To blow the King and Parliament
All up alive.
Threescore barrels, laid below,
To prove old England's overthrow.
But, by God's providence, him they catch,
With a dark lantern, lighting a match!
A stick and a stake
For King James's sake!
If you won't give me one,
I'll take two,
The better for me,
And the worse for you.
A rope, a rope, to hang the Pope,
A penn'orth of cheese to choke him,
A pint of beer to wash it down,
And a jolly good fire to burn him.
Holloa, boys! holloa, boys! make the bells ring!
Holloa, boys! holloa boys! God save the King!
Hip, hip, hooor-r-r-ray!

John Milton, "On the Fifth of November," 1626

1630, BEAR-BAITING

Bear-baiting was a popular spectacle in the Tudor and Stuart period, along with similarly gruesome sports such as dogfights and cockfights. Animal blood sports appealed to many theatergoers at the time, and two of the most famous bear pits were located in south London, close to Shakespeare's Globe.

I went with some friends to the Bear Garden, where was cock-fighting, dog-fighting, bear and bull-baiting, it being a famous day for all these butcherly sports, or rather barbarous cruelties. The bulls did exceedingly well, but the Irish wolf dog exceeded, which was a tall greyhound, a stately creature indeed, who beat a cruel mastiff. One of the bulls tossed a dog full into a lady's lap as she sat in one of the boxes at a considerable height from the arena. Two poor dogs were killed, and so all ended with the ape on horseback, and I most heartily weary of the rude and dirty pastime, which I had not seen, I think, in twenty years before.

John Evelyn, The Diary of John Evelyn,
in the entry for June 16, 1670

NEWES

SACKE & SUGAR

JARMARA

VINEGAR TOM

1640s, THE WITCH TEST

MATTHEW HOPKINS

Matthew Hopkins was an English witch-hunter whose fame grew during the English Civil War, earning him the title Witch Finder General. His torturous methods included the swimming test, which entailed binding an accused woman and throwing her into water. It was postulated that if she floated rather than sank, she was confirmed to be a witch.

This singular character, known as Mother Damnable, is also called Mother Red Cap, and sometimes the Shrew of Kentish Town. . . .

She was resorted to by numbers as a fortune-teller and healer of strange diseases; and when any mishap occurred, then the old crone was set upon by the mob and hooted without mercy. The old, ill-favoured creature would at such times lean out of her hatch-door, with a grotesque red cap on her head. She had a large broad nose, heavy, shaggy eyebrows, sunken eyes, and lank and leathern cheeks; her forehead wrinkled, her mouth wide, and her looks sullen and unmoved. On her shoulders was thrown a dark grey striped frieze, with black patches, which looked at a distance like flying bats. Suddenly she would let her huge black cat jump upon the hatch by her side, when the mob instantly retreated from a superstitious dread of the double foe.

Samuel Palmer, St. Pancras; Being Antiquarian, Topographical, and Biographical Memoranda, Relating to the Extensive Metropolitan Parish of St. Pancras, Middlesex: with Some Account of the Parish from Its Foundation, *1870*

1642-1651, THE CIVIL WAR

Charles I's actions had sown division throughout the country, leading to the Civil War, which pitted king against Parliament: the Royalist Cavaliers against the Parliamentarian Roundheads.

During the fighting, a notable battle formation was the "hedgehog." When enemy cavalry attacked, Roundhead soldiers created a hedgehog shape, with the musketeers in the middle and the pikemen around the edges.

1649, CHARLES I EXECUTED

Charles I was defeated, taken prisoner by the Parliamentarians, and eventually brought to trial for treason. The King, sentenced to death by beheading, remains the only English monarch to have been executed.

Oliver Cromwell, one of the fifty-nine members of Parliament to sign the king's death warrant, permitted the king's head to be sewn back onto his body, allowing his family to pay their last respects before Charles I's burial.

There was such a groan by the thousands then present as I never heard before and desire I may never hear again.

Philip Henry, a witness to Charles I's execution, 1649

1640s, CHRISTMAS BEFORE CROMWELL

Christmas was a wild celebration during the Stuart period. It lasted for many days and included feasts and outrageous games.

1653, CHRISTMAS UNDER CROMWELL

After Oliver Cromwell became Lord Protector of the Commonwealth, Parliament offered him the crown in 1657 but Cromwell refused.

Cromwell and his largely Puritanical Parliament enforced a more austere lifestyle and manner of worship on many Londoners. Soldiers were given authority to close theaters, inns, and pubs before Parliament passed an ordinance banning the celebration of Christmas in 1647. The ban had varying degrees of success in the following years.

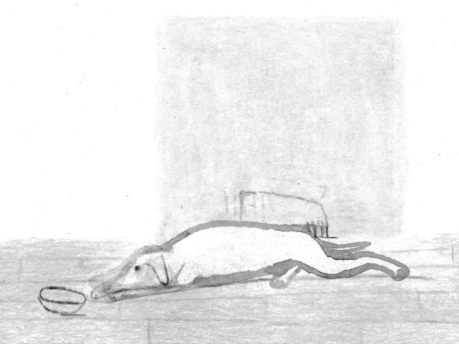

1660, CHARLES II AND THE RESTORATION*

Parliament invited Charles II back from exile and restored him to the throne, ending the Interregnum period, when Parliamentarians governed the country. The king arrived in London on his thirtieth birthday and went back to live in his boyhood home, the Palace of Whitehall.

In revenge for his father's death, Charles II ordered that Oliver Cromwell's body be dug up. His corpse was hung in chains before being beheaded. His severed head was displayed outside Westminster Hall.

1665-1666,
THE GREAT PLAGUE

Seventeenth-century London was a densely packed, unsanitary place with a high death rate, so when the bubonic plague revisited the city, the first fatalities drew little interest. Symptoms included high fevers, headaches, and painful swellings. The plague usually resulted in death.

Death rates increased over the hot summer months. Local authorities were charged with preventing the spread of the disease. They organized watchmen to stand guard outside infected households and oversee the burial of bodies in plague pits.

The plague transformed London into a strange, quiet place; the bustling markets were closed, the Thames was empty of its usual traffic, and people were forced to stay in their homes. It is estimated that London lost around one-fifth of its population.

To be observed by all Justices of Peace, Mayors, Bayliffs, and other Officers, for prevention of the spreading of the Infection of the PLAGUE.

Published by His Majesties [*sic*] Special Command.

7. That care be taken that no unwholsom [*sic*] Meats, stinking Fish, Flesh, musty Corn, or any other unwholsome [*sic*] Food be exposed to sale in any Shops or Markets.

8. That no Swine, Dogs, Cats, or tame Pigeons be permitted to pass up and down in Streets, or from house to house, in places Infected.

9. That the Laws against Inn-Mates be forthwith put in strict execution, and that no more Alehouses be Licensed then [*sic*] are absolutely necessary in each City or place, especially during the continuance of this present Contagion.

10. That each City and Town forthwith provide some convenient place remote from the same, where a Pest-house, Huts, or Sheds may be Erected, to be in readiness in case any Infection should break out; which if it shall happen to do, That able and faithful Searchers and Examiners be forthwith provided and Sworn to Search all suspected bodies, for the usual signs of the Plague, viz. Swellings or Risings under the Ears or Arm-pits, or upon the Groynes [groin]; Blains [sores], Carbuncles, or little Spots, either on the Breast or back, commonly called Tokens.

11. That if any House be Infected, the sick person or persons be forthwith removed to the said Pest-house, Sheds, or Huts, for the preservation of the rest of the Family: And that such house (though none be dead therein) be shut up for Fourty [*sic*] days, and have a Red Cross, and Lord have mercy upon us, in Capital Letters affixed on the door, and Warders appointed, as well to find them necessaries, as to keep them from conversing with the sound.

Orders for the Prevention of the Plague, 1666

1666,
THE GREAT FIRE

The Great Fire of London began in the king's bakery in Pudding Lane. A long, dry summer, strong winds, and the close proximity of so many wooden buildings led to the flames spreading swiftly.

The mayor was called but he dismissed the severity of the blaze, stating, "Pish! A woman might piss it out." The fire blazed for four days and destroyed 13,000 houses, leaving over 70,000 people homeless.

By and by Jane comes and tells me that she hears that above 300 houses have been burned down to-night by the fire we saw, and that it is now burning down all Fish-street, by London Bridge. So I made myself ready presently, and walked to the Tower, and there got up upon one of the high places, ... and there I did see the houses at that end of the bridge all on fire, and an infinite great fire on this and the other side the end of the bridge. . . . So down, with my heart full of trouble, to the Lieutenant of the Tower, who tells me that it begun this morning in the King's baker's house in Pudding-lane, and that it hath burned St. Magnus's Church and most part of Fish-street already. So I down to the water-side, and there got a boat and through bridge, and there saw a lamentable fire. . . . Everybody endeavouring to remove their goods, and flinging into the river or bringing them into lighters that layoff; poor people staying in their houses as long as till the very fire touched them, and then running into boats, or clambering from one pair of stairs by the water-side to another. And among other things, the poor pigeons, I perceive, were loth to leave their houses, but hovered about the windows and balconys till they were, some of them burned, their wings, and fell down.

Samuel Pepys, The Diary of Samuel Pepys, *in the entry for September 2, 1666*

Oh, the miserable and calamitous spectacle! . . . All the sky was of a fiery aspect, like the top of a burning oven, and the light seen above forty miles round about for many nights. God grant mine eyes may never behold the like, who now saw above 10,000 houses all in one flame! The noise and cracking and thunder of the impetuous flames, the shrieking of women and children, the hurry of people, the fall of towers, houses, and churches, was like a hideous storm; and the air all about so hot and inflamed, that at the last one was not able to approach it, so that they were forced to stand still, and let the flames burn on, which they did, for near two miles in length and one in breadth. . . . London was, but is no more!

John Evelyn, The Diary of John Evelyn, *in the entry for September 3, 1666*

Thomas Farynor, Baker to the King,
Left his oven burning with the firewood nearby.
The embers muttered, the little flames took wing
And sang to the bigger flames, Come with us and fly!

So fly they did, from the Baker to The Star,
To The Star next door in Fish street, in one almighty flap,
From there on to St Margaret's which wasn't very far,
The little flames kept hopping from one gap to narrow gap.

Here lay the tallow, the spirits and the straw,
Here lay the coal and the hemp and the oil,
Given a decent breeze the fire began to draw,
And soon barrels full of water were coming to the boil.

How happy were the flames, the gleeful little pests,
They sang and crowed and whistled in full throat,
Flashing now their wings and now their bright red breasts,
Like robins who had never sung a note.

By now their bigger cousins were roosting on the bridge,
Old London Bridge was burning and the Thames was molten lead,
But the firebirds kept leaping the gap from ridge to ridge,
Till the city blazed from the roof to riverbed.

Oh it was spectacular, those flames up to their tricks,
And the mess they left behind them was desolate and vague.
For days they screeched and bellowed in 1666,
And wiped away whole districts, but also purged the Plague,

Or so they told each other when the squawking had died down,
And whether it was accident or fate
They certainly had changed the face of the whole town
Before they settled back into the grate.

George Szirtes, "The Great Fire of London,"
In the Land of the Giants, *2012*

1671, REBUILDING LONDON: A MONUMENT

It took around fifty years to rebuild London after the Great Fire. New regulations mandated that buildings had to be constructed of brick and stone.

A group of six, including architect Sir Christopher Wren, was entrusted with restoring London. As part of the project, the Monument to the Great Fire was erected, beginning in 1671. The imposing Doric column stands 200 feet (61 meters) high—the exact distance between it and the site in Pudding Lane where the fire began.

Two sticks and an apple,
Ring the bells at Whitechapel.

Old Father Bald Pate,
Ring the bells Aldgate.

Maids in white aprons,
Ring the bells at St. Catherine's.

Oranges and lemons,
Ring the bells at St. Clement's.

When will you pay me?
Ring the bells at the Old Bailey.

When I am rich,
Ring the bells at Fleetditch.

When will that be?
Ring the bells of Stepney.

When I am old,
Ring the great bell at Paul's.

Anonymous, "London Bells,"
early eighteenth century

1675, THE NEW SAINT PAUL'S CATHEDRAL

The rebuilding of Saint Paul's Cathedral spanned forty years, with the groundbreaking taking place in 1675. The appointed architect, Sir Christopher Wren, had a large stone phoenix placed in the pediment on the south side. It stands above the word RESURGAM, Latin for "I will rise again." It symbolized London rising from the ashes of the Great Fire.

Sir Christopher Wren
Said: "I am going to dine with some men.
If anyone calls
Say I am designing St. Paul's."

Edmund Clerihew Bentley,
Biography for Beginners, *1905*

And high above this winding length of street,
This noiseless and unpeopled avenue,
Pure, silent, solemn, beautiful, was seen
The huge majestic Temple of St Paul
In awful sequestration, through a veil,
Through its own sacred veil of falling snow.

William Wordsworth, "St Paul's," 1808

1675, THE GREENWICH OBSERVATORY*

King Charles II commissioned Sir Christopher Wren to design the Royal Observatory in 1675. It is Britain's oldest and first state-funded scientific institution.

Whereas, in order to the finding out of the longitude of places for perfecting navigation and astronomy, we have resolved to build a small observatory within our park at Greenwich, upon the highest ground, at or near the place where the castle stood, with lodging-rooms for our astronomical observator and assistant. Our will and pleasure is, that according to such plot and design as shall be given you by our trusty and well-beloved Sir Christopher Wren, Knight, our surveyor-general of the place and scite [*sic*] of the said observatory, you cause the same to be fenced in, built and finished with all convenient speed, by such artificers and workmen as you shall appoint thereto.

Charles II, The warrant for building the Royal Observatory in Greenwich, 1675

1683–1684, FROST FAIR*

Between 1600 and 1814, a section of the Thames regularly froze for up to two months at a time. Some years, including in the winter of 1683–1684, frost fairs took place on the ice, delighting many Londoners.

Coaches plied from Westminster to the Temple, and from several other stairs to and fro, as in the streets, sleds, sliding with skates, a bull-baiting, horse and coach-races, puppet-plays and interludes, cooks, tippling, and other lewd places, so that it seemed to be a bacchanalian triumph, or carnival on the water . . . and the very seas so locked up with ice, that no vessels could stir out or come in.

John Evelyn, The Diary of John Evelyn, *in the entry for January 24, 1684*

1690s, COFFEEHOUSES

Coffeehouses in London were new exciting places for socializing, intellectual discussions, and doing business. They catered solely to men, including politicians, writers, and scientists.

One snowy day late in December—(the sun, I well recollect, was just disappearing behind the tower of the old Exchange)—I went with him, for the first time, to that famous coffee-house. . . . Entering the wide, low-roofed coffee-room, we found nearly every box and seat occupied, but at length discovered a vacant recess, where we two (I was but a little one) secured places. My conductor, doubtless divining my thoughts, said, "You can call for what you like." My most pressing wish was for a muffin from the little legion so pleasantly browning at the fire. What a tremendous, capacious grate it seemed! and all the bars were red-hot. "Waiter, coffee and a muffin." Sam responded most cordially. In less than ten minutes I made a second demand, and nothing but some lingering remains of boyish modesty prevented me asking for a third muffin. The muffins of that day were certainly far superior to the muffins of 1862; indeed, my private opinion is that even the crumpets we now consume, though so neatly shaped, are by no means equal to those that took any shape they pleased on the ovens of Hanway-yard. A bell rings; coffee and stronger beverages are deserted—all ascend the broad, centre stair, to the sale-room. Folks seemed in admirable humour; sly jokes were circulating from ear to ear; everybody appeared to know everybody; and the auctioneer was so cordially greeted on ascending his rostrum that you might have fancied the wood was to be had as a gift, instead of a purchase.

Aleph, "Garraway's Coffee-House,"
London Scenes and London People, *1863*

1703,
BUCKINGHAM PALACE*

Buckingham Palace was originally Buckingham House, a three-floored townhouse built by the Duke of Buckingham in 1703. King George III, who found Saint James's Palace lacking in privacy, bought the house for his wife, Queen Charlotte. It became known as the Queen's House.

George IV, son of George III, employed the architect John Nash to transform the building into a palace. However, he never moved in and Queen Victoria was the first monarch to live there.

As for our Buckingham Palace yesterday—never was there such a specimen of wicked, vulgar profusion. It has cost a million of money, and there is not a fault that has not been committed in it. You may be sure there are rooms enough, and large enough, for the money; but for staircases, passages, &c., I observed that instead of being called Buckingham Palace, it should be the "Brunswick Hotel." The costly ornaments of the state rooms exceed all belief in their bad taste and every species of infirmity. Raspberry-coloured pillars without end, that quite turn you sick to look at; but the Queen's paper for her own apartments far exceed everything else in their ugliness and vulgarity.

Thomas Creevey, in a letter to Elizabeth Ord, 1835

1720s, LONDON BRIDGE

London Bridge has existed since the Romans
ruled the city and has been updated and rebuilt
throughout history. Shops once lined both sides
of the bridge, causing crowding and congestion
on the narrow road that passed between them.
To reduce the chaos, in the 1720s, vehicles were
instructed to keep to the left, a requirement
that would eventually become the rule of the
road in Britain.

1735, NUMBER 10 GIVEN TO THE PRIME MINISTER

King George II offered three houses to Robert Walpole, who is usually regarded as the first British prime minister. Walpole commissioned the architect William Kent to join them into the larger house known as Number 10 Downing Street.

The house was built using yellow bricks, but they gradually became darker due to London's pollution. The bricks are now painted black.

1738, GIN*

In the eighteenth century, gin was cheap and readily available, and, for many Londoners, it offered an escape from the misery of their daily lives.

Gin cursed Friend, with Fury fraught,
 Makes human race a Prey;
It enters by a deadly Draught,
 And steals our Life away.
Virtue and Truth, driv'n to Despair,
 Its Rage compells to fly,
But cherishes, with hellish Care,
 Theft, Murder, Perjury.
Damn'd Cup! that on the vitals preys,
 That liquid Fire contains
Which madness to the Heart Conveys
 And rolls it thro' the Veins.

Rev. James Townley, "Gin," 1751

1739, THE FOUNDLING HOSPITAL

Despite London's thriving industry, many people still lived in extreme poverty; children and babies were left especially vulnerable, causing the child mortality rate to be alarmingly high. Nearly two-thirds of children died by the age of five.

Captain Thomas Coram was appalled to see babies dying on London's streets, and in response, he established the Foundling Hospital, dedicated to the care and education of abandoned children. The artist William Hogarth and the composer George Frideric Handel were early supporters of Coram; they helped to raise funds, and Handel held benefit concerts of *Messiah* in the hospital's chapel that proved very popular.

Mothers left their babies in the hospital's care but retained the hope of being reunited with their children. They often left a small token, to be kept in the hospital archive along with the child's paperwork, as a means of identification.

1762,
A SPERM WHALE
IN LONDON

London was once a busy, thriving whaling port. When a large sperm whale carcass was dragged to Greenland Dock, in order to process the body for oil and meat, inquisitive Londoners gathered to watch the spectacle, despite the offensive stench.

1737-1777,
A VIEW ACROSS
MARYLEBONE GARDENS

London was growing, but outside the city,
Marylebone was still a quiet village surrounded
by fields. As society prospered, the Marylebone
Pleasure Gardens opened for socializing, with bear-
baiting and duels taking place in Marylebone Fields.

Charles Wesley, Methodist cleric and poet, lived
and worked in Marylebone. He could be seen riding
his white pony while wearing his trademark blue
coat and wide-brimmed hat. He composed numerous
hymns, including "Love Divine, All Loves Excelling"
and "Hark! The Herald Angels Sing."

1768, THE OPENING OF THE ROYAL ACADEMY

With the approval of King George III, a group of artists and architects founded the Royal Academy of Arts, with the purpose of "promoting the Arts of Design." The Royal Academy's events gained huge popularity, and their summer exhibitions have been held annually since 1769.

1780, DUTIES OF A HOUSEMAID

The rise of successful merchants and gentry in London brought a more luxurious lifestyle to the city. They lived in mansions filled with extravagant furniture and exquisite porcelain and pottery. There were exciting new foods and drinks to try, including tea and coffee. Wealthy households employed servants, including at least one housemaid.

A housemaid should be active, clean, and neat in her person; an early riser; of a respectful and steady deportment, and possessed of a temper that will not be easily ruffled. She must be able to see, without much appearance of discomposure, her labours often increased by the carelessness and thoughtlessness of others. Many a dirty foot will obtrude itself upon her clean floors; and the well-polished furniture will demand her strength and patience, when spotted or soiled by some reckless hand.

Mrs William Parkes, Domestic Duties: or, Instructions to Young Married Ladies, on the Management of Their Households, and the Regulation of Their Conduct in the Various Relations and Duties of Married Life, *1829*

1780, THE GORDON RIOTS

The Catholic Relief Act of 1778 sparked a great deal of anti-Catholic feeling, leading to days of rioting and looting across London. The Gordon Riots are considered by some to be the closest Britain has ever come to a full-blown revolution.

At night they set fire to the Fleet, and to the King's Bench, and I know not how many other places; and one might see the glare of conflagration fill the sky from many parts. The sight was dreadful. Some people were threatened; Mr Strahan advised me to take care of myself. Such a time of terror you have been happy in not seeing.

James Boswell, The Life of Samuel Johnson, *1791*

1794, DANDIES*

Etonian George "Beau" Brummell was a close friend of the Prince of Wales and heavily influenced the prince and his circle. Brummell displayed keen social awareness, and his personal style and revolutionary grooming practices popularized the term "dandy."

First, touching Dandies, let us consider, with some scientific strictness, what a Dandy specially is. A Dandy is a Clothes-wearing Man, a Man whose trade, office, and existence consists in the wearing of Clothes. Every faculty of his soul, spirit, purse and person is heroically consecrated to this one object, the wearing of Clothes wisely and well: so that as others dress to live, he lives to dress.

Thomas Carlyle, "The Dandiacal Body," Sartor Resartus, *1836*

1800s, THE INDUSTRIAL REVOLUTION

Increasing industrialization widened the wealth gap between rich and poor, and brought people from the country to the city to work in factories. London's population doubled as a result.

I wander thro' each charter'd street,
Near where the charter'd Thames does flow.
And mark in every face I meet
Marks of weakness, marks of woe.

In every cry of every Man,
In every Infants cry of fear,
In every voice: in every ban,
The mind-forg'd manacles I hear

How the Chimney-sweepers cry
Every blackning Church appalls,
And the hapless Soldiers sigh
Runs in blood down Palace walls

But most thro' midnight streets I hear
How the youthful Harlots curse
Blasts the new-born Infants tear
And blights with plagues the Marriage hearse

William Blake, "London," Songs of Innocence and Experience, *1794*

1834, WESTMINSTER FIRE

In October 1834, a fire destroyed much of the Palace of Westminster, which housed Parliament. The fire started in the Exchequer's office, where wooden tally sticks were being burned in a stove. The blaze was an extraordinary sight and attracted many onlookers. J. M. W. Turner was one of the many artists who painted the event.

"[The fire was] the greatest instance of stupidity on record."

Lord Melbourne, in the subsequent inquiry, 1834

1838, THE RAILWAYS

As railways were being built in the 1800s, the fact that there was no standard time across Britain became problematic. Oxford, for instance, was five minutes behind London. This inconsistency played havoc with train timetables and meant people missed connections. It was also feared that trains using different local times would arrive at the same station simultaneously, resulting in crashes. Eventually, rail companies all switched to London time and in 1880, time was finally standardized across the country.

1843, NELSON'S COLUMN BUILT IN TRAFALGAR SQUARE

Vice Admiral Lord Horatio Nelson died while fighting the French at the Battle of Trafalgar in 1805. This was such a significant victory for the English and Nelson was so admired that a column was erected to commemorate his life.

The column is 160 feet (51.6 meters) tall and, when it was built, could be seen all over London. The four bronze relief panels at the sides were cast from melted-down French guns.

Nelson's body was brought home from his flagship HMS Victory and buried in Saint Paul's Cathedral. His uniform was preserved and displayed at the National Maritime Museum.

His Nation's bulwark, and all Nature's pride,
The Hero liv'd, and as he liv'd—he died—
Transcendent Destiny! how blest the brave
Whose fall his Country's tears attend, shower'd on his
     trophied grave!

Thomas Gent, "On the Death of Lord Nelson," 1808

1850, VICTORIAN STREET LIFE*

Henry Mayhew was a journalist who documented and wrote about working people in London for the *Morning Chronicle*. The articles, which showed the fragility of life for many in the world's richest city, were later collected into a book, *London Labour and the London Poor*.

"I was fifteen on the 24th of last May, sir, and I've been sweeping crossings now near upon two years. . . .

 . . . When we gets home at half-past three in the morning, whoever cries out 'first wash' has it. First of all we washes our feet, and we all uses the same water. Then we washes our faces and hands, and necks, and whoever fetches the fresh water up has first wash; and if the second don't like to go get fresh, why he uses the dirty." [Crossing-sweeper]

"I go about the streets with water-creases [*sic*], crying, 'Four bunches a penny, water-creases.' . . .

 . . . I knows a good many games, but I don't play at 'em, 'cos going out with creases tires me. . . . I aint [*sic*] a child, and I shan't be a woman till I'm twenty, but I'm past eight, I am." [Watercress girl]

The pavement and the road are crowded with purchasers and street-sellers. The housewife in her thick shawl, with the market-basket on her arm, walks slowly on, stopping now to look at the stall of caps, and now to cheapen a bunch of greens. Little boys, holding three or four onions in their hand, creep between the people, wriggling their way through every interstice, and asking for custom in whining tones, as if seeking charity. Then the tumult of the thousand different cries of the eager dealers, all shouting at the top of their voices, at one and the same time, is almost bewildering. "So-old again," roars one. "Chestnuts all 'ot, a penny a score," bawls another. "An 'aypenny a skin, blacking," squeaks a boy. "Buy, buy, buy, buy, buy—bu-u-uy!" cries the butcher. "Half-quire of paper for a penny," bellows the street stationer. . . . "Twopence a pound grapes." . . . "Who'll buy a bonnet for fourpence?" . . . "Now's your time! beautiful whelks, a penny a lot." . . . "Come and look at 'em! here's toasters!" bellows one with a Yarmouth bloater stuck on a toasting-fork. "Penny a lot, fine russets," calls the apple woman: and so the Babel goes on.

Henry Mayhew, London Labour and the London Poor, *1851*

1851,
THE GREAT
EXHIBITION*

As industrialization progressed rapidly in Britain, the Great Exhibition of the Works of Industry of All Nations was held in London's Hyde Park to display manufactured products from all over the world. This spectacular event, organized by Prince Albert and Henry Cole, brought visitors to marvel at the wonders of industry.

152

The Exhibition is indeed amazing. You feel the terrible force which has brought these innumerable people, who had come from the ends of the earth all together into one fold; you realize the grandeur of the idea; you feel that something has been achieved here, that here is victory and triumph. And you feel nervous. However great your independence of mind, a feeling of fear somehow creeps over you. . . .

. . . You look at those hundreds of thousands, at those millions of people obediently trooping into this place from all parts of the earth—people who have come with only one thought, quietly, stubbornly and silently milling round in this colossal palace; and you feel that something final has been accomplished here—accomplished and completed. It is a biblical sight, something to do with Babylon, some prophecy out of the Apocalypse being fulfilled before your very eyes.

Fyodor Dostoevsky, Winter Notes on Summer Impressions, *1863*

1852, POLITICS: NEW HOUSES OF PARLIAMENT BUILT

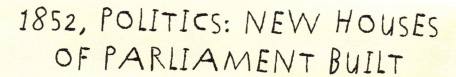

The new Houses of Parliament, which took over thirty years to build, were designed by the architect Charles Barry, in collaboration with Augustus Pugin. By 1852, both the Lords and the Commons were able to occupy their respective chambers.

[It was] without doubt the finest specimen of gothic civil architecture in Europe: its proportions, arrangement, and decoration being perfect, and worthy of the great nation at whose cost it has been erected.

The Illustrated London News, *April 17, 1847*

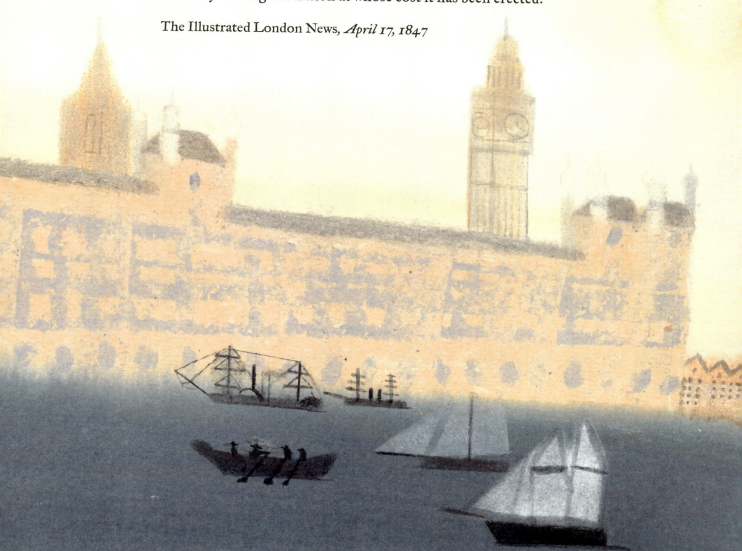

1854, THE CRYSTAL PALACE DINOSAURS

A selection of dinosaur sculptures was commissioned for the Crystal Palace after it was moved from the Great Exhibition in Hyde Park to Sydenham Hill. Although now known to be inaccurate, they were the first attempt at full-scale dinosaur statues in the world and reflected the latest scientific knowledge at the time.

Before the dinosaurs were unveiled to the public, the sculptor Benjamin Waterhouse Hawkins hosted a dinner in the mold of one of the *Iguanodon* sculptures.

The Restoration of the Iguanodon was one of the largest and earliest completed of Mr Waterhouse Hawkins' gigantic models measuring thirty feet from the nose to the end of the tail, of that quantity the body with the neck contained about fifteen feet which when the pieces of the mould that formed the ridge of the back were removed the body presented the appearance of a wide open Boot with on [*sic*] enclosed arch seven feet high at both ends.

"*The Dinner in the Mould of the Iguanodon,*" The Illustrated London News, *January 7, 1854*

1855,
TRANSPORT*

London's narrow, winding streets thronged with
people, bicycles, carts, and even horse buses.

1858, THE GREAT STINK

For centuries, waste was discharged into the river Thames, and by the hot summer of 1858, it had created a dire problem. The repugnant smell, known as the "Great Stink," forced politicians to allow the development of a new sewage system, created by Sir Joseph William Bazalgette.

SIR, I traversed this day by steam-boat the space between London and Hangerford [*sic*] Bridges between half-past one and two o'clock; it was low water, and I think the tide must have been near the turn. The appearance and the smell of the water forced themselves at once on my attention. The whole of the river was an opaque pale brown fluid. In order to test the degree of opacity, I tore up some white cards into pieces, moistened them so as to make them sink easily below the surface, and then dropped some of these pieces into the water at every pier the boat came to; before they had sunk an inch below the surface they were indistinguishable, though the sun shone brightly at the time; and when the pieces fell edgeways the lower part was hidden from sight before the upper part was under water. This happened at St. Paul's Wharf, Blackfriars Bridge, Temple Wharf, Southwark Bridge, and Hungerford; and I have no doubt would have occurred further up and down the river. Near the bridges the feculence rolled up in clouds so dense that they were visible at the surface, even in water of this kind.

Professor Michael Faraday, "Observations on the Filth of the Thames,"
a letter in the Times *(London), July 7, 1855*

1860s, A MAP OF VICTORIAN LONDON*

The Industrial Revolution led to a huge increase in the urban population, which in London rose to three million. This brought about a period of significant change and development in the city and society.

In the country, the rain would have developed a thousand fresh scents, and every drop would have had its bright association with some beautiful form of growth or life. In the city, it developed only foul stale smells, and was a sickly, lukewarm, dirt-stained, wretched addition to the gutters.

Charles Dickens, Little Dorrit, 1857

1863, UNDERGROUND

When the Metropolitan Railway opened in 1863, trains ran every fifteen minutes in each direction during off-peak hours. People moved to live and work near the stations.

The first shock of a great earthquake had, just at that period, rent the whole neighbourhood to its centre. Traces of its course were visible on every side. Houses were knocked down; streets broken through and stopped; deep pits and trenches dug in the ground; enormous heaps of earth and clay thrown up; buildings that were undermined and shaking, propped by great beams of wood.

Charles Dickens, Dombey and Son, *1848*

1881, THE NATURAL HISTORY MUSEUM

The Natural History Museum was built in
South Kensington to house the natural history
collections that were originally kept in the
British Museum. Sir Richard Owen, the first
superintendent of the Natural History Museum,
argued for the importance of dedicating a
separate space to these specimens. He called it a
"cathedral to nature" and was determined that
the building would have the capacity to display
even the largest of creatures: the blue whale.

1886, TOWER BRIDGE

The City of London Corporation held a public competition to design a new crossing over the Thames in 1876. The winning entry, by Horace Jones and John Wolfe Barry, was chosen years after the contest was launched. Their bridge now spans two different London boroughs, with the North Tower in Tower Hamlets and the South Tower in Southwark.

Before we knew it, we were going across Tower Bridge but just as we had gone over the first half of the section that goes up there was aloud [*sic*] crashing sound and I was thrown onto the floor. The bus came to a halt and the driver came round to invite us to have a look at the gap that had opened on the opposite half. The driver then told us that as he started to drive across the opening part of the bridge, he realised that the side that the bus was on was going up.

He said he could only think of two options as to what to do: one was to stop the bus and hope someone would realise what was happening and stop it, but that left the possibility of the bus slipping back and perhaps toppling into the river; the other was to continue driving and to "jump" the gap. He said that he had been a tank-driver during the war and that a tank would have had no trouble getting onto the other side and decided to see if a double-decker could do the same. So, to his quick thinking, we were all delivered safe to the other side.

Account of an incident when a London bus jumped Tower Bridge, December 20, 1952

169

1898, HARRODS' FIRST ESCALATOR

The London department store
Harrods showcased the city's first
"moving staircase," a contraption
made from woven leather that
functioned like an inclined
conveyor belt. It generated much
excitement among customers.

Installed in Harrods in 1898 because
the manager had an intense dislike of
lifts, the first escalator proved such
a moving experience for many who
rode on it that an attendant had to be
stationed at the top to dispense brandy
or sal volatile respectively to gentlemen
or ladies overcome by terror. When
the first escalator at an underground
station was opened at Earls Court in
1911, the District Railway engaged
"Bumper" Harris, a man with a wooden
leg, to ride up and down it all day to
instil confidence in the faint-hearted.

Russell Ash, The Londoner's
Almanac, *1985*

VOTES FOR WOM
VOTES FOR WOMEN
VOTES FOR WOMEN MEETING WOMEN DEMAND THE VOTE
WOME DEMAND THE VOT THIS SESSION

1906, THE WOMEN'S SUFFRAGE MOVEMENT

Emmeline Pankhurst was a leader of the women's suffrage movement in Britain, fighting for the right of women to vote. Her group, the Women's Social and Political Union, was founded in Manchester and moved its headquarters to London in 1906, to be near the seat of government. They campaigned relentlessly and their tactics included attacks on property and artworks, heckling members of Parliament, and staging protests.

I know that women, once convinced that they are doing what is right, that their rebellion is just, will go on, no matter what the difficulties, no matter what the dangers, so long as there is a woman alive to hold up the flag of rebellion.

Emmeline Pankhurst, in a public speech, 1913

OVERLEAF

1908, DOUBLE-DECKER BUS

1914, WORLD WAR I *

In response to Germany's occupation of Belgium, Britain entered World War I on August 4, 1914.

"When you are a soldier you are one of two things, either at the front or behind the lines. If you are behind the lines you need not worry. If you are at the front you are one of two things. You are either in a danger zone or in a zone which is not dangerous. If you are in a zone which is not dangerous you need not worry. If you are in a danger zone you are one of two things; either you are wounded or you are not. If you are not wounded you need not worry. If you are wounded you are one of two things, either seriously wounded or slightly wounded. If you are slightly wounded you need not worry. If you are seriously wounded one of two things is certain—either you get well or you die. If you get well you needn't worry. If you die you cannot worry, so there is no need to worry about anything at all."

Vera Brittain quoting her uncle, in Testament of Youth, *1933*

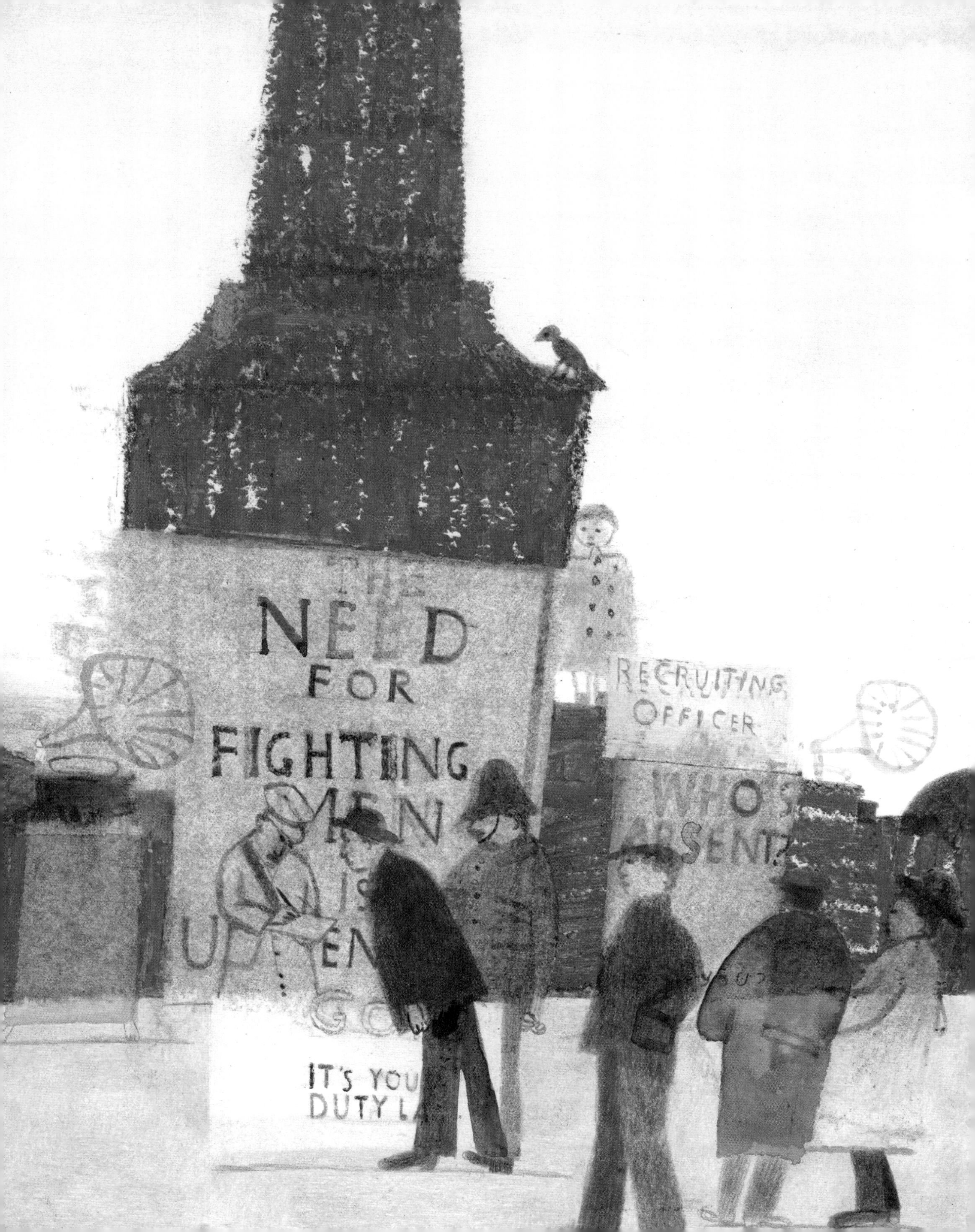
NEED FOR FIGHTING MEN
RECRUITING OFFICER
IT'S YOU
DUTY L

1915,
THE FIRST AIR RAID

On May 31, 1915, for the first time in centuries, London was attacked. A German Zeppelin airship, using the river Thames as a guide, drifted silently toward East London. It dropped ninety bombs and thirty grenades on the city.

If you had been with me last Wednesday you could have watched the Zeppelins and the guns firing at it—as if from a private box. It was a dark night with a few stars, and the Zeppelins stood out very clearly in the searchlights. The firing went on for 20 minutes or so—many guns to the minute, mostly falling short but a few very close, and gradually it got out of range. London seemed very still, a dog could be heard barking far away; it was eerie waiting.

J. M. Barrie, in a letter to Charles Scribner, 1915

THE LORD KNOWETH THEM THAT ARE HIS

BENEATH THIS STONE RESTS THE BODY
OF A BRITISH WARRIOR
UNKNOWN BY NAME OR RANK
BROUGHT FROM FRANCE TO LIE AMONG
THE MOST ILLUSTRIOUS OF THE LAND
AND BURIED HERE ON ARMISTICE DAY
11 NOV: 1920. IN THE PRESENCE OF

HIS MAJESTY KING GEORGE V
HIS MINISTERS OF STATE
THE CHIEFS OF HIS FORCES

AND A VAST CONCOURSE OF THE NATION

THUS ARE COMMEMORATED THE MANY
MULTITUDES WHO DURING THE GREAT
WAR OF 1914-1918 GAVE THE MOST THAT
MAN CAN GIVE LIFE ITSELF
FOR GOD
FOR KING AND COUNTRY
FOR LOVED ONES HOME AND EMPIRE
FOR THE SACRED CAUSE OF JUSTICE AND
THE FREEDOM OF THE WORLD

THEY BURIED HIM AMONG THE KINGS BECAUSE HE
HAD DONE GOOD TOWARD GOD AND TOWARD
HIS HOUSE

IN CHRIST SHALL ALL BE MADE ALIVE

GREATER LOVE HATH NO MAN THAN THIS

UNKNOWN AND YET WELL KNOWN, DYING AND BEHOLD WE LIVE

1920,
THE TOMB OF
THE UNKNOWN
WARRIOR

Millions of soldiers died in World War I.
The Tomb of the Unknown Warrior was created
in Westminster Abbey to honor all those who
died in British service and whose bodies were
never found.

The tomb contains the remains of an
unidentified British serviceman who died on
the battlefield. His grave is one of Britain's most
important war memorials.

The Cenotaph, it may be said, is the token of our
mourning as a nation; the Grave of the Unknown
Warrior is the token of our mourning as individuals.

David Lloyd George, in a letter to David Lutyens, 1920

1920s, BRINGING IN SHEEP TO CUT THE GRASS

In the 1920s, sheep were often brought into London parks as "natural lawnmowers."

1939, WORLD WAR II*

Following Germany's invasion of Poland, Britain entered World War II on September 3, 1939. Soon, Hitler's air force began a relentless bombing campaign, which came to be known as the Blitz, against London and other British cities.

I am speaking to you from the cabinet room at 10 Downing Street. This morning the British ambassador in Berlin handed the German government a final note stating that unless we heard from them by 11 o'clock that they were prepared at once to withdraw their troops from Poland, a state of war would exist between us. I have to tell you now that no such undertaking has been received, and that consequently this country is at war with Germany.

*British prime minister Neville Chamberlain,
in a radio broadcast, September 3, 1939*

1940–1941, THE BLITZ*

The term *Blitz* comes from the German word *Blitzkrieg* (lightning war). The campaign began on September 7, 1940, with a bombing raid on London that left 430 dead and 1,600 injured. The attacks continued for fifty-seven consecutive nights. The city was bombed more heavily and frequently than anywhere else in Britain.

London raises her head, shakes the debris of the night from her hair, and takes stock of the damage done. London has been damaged during the night. The sign of a great fighter in the ring is: can he get up from the floor after being knocked down?

London does this every morning. London doesn't look down upon the ruins of its houses, of those made homeless during the night, upon the remains of churches, hospitals, workers' flats. London looks upwards t'ward the dawn and faces the new day with calmness and confidence.

The peoples' army go to work as they did in that other comfortable world which came to an end when the invader began to attack the last strongholds of freedom.

Not all the services run as they did yesterday. But London manages to get to work on time. One way or another. In the centre of the city the shops are open as usual. In fact many of them are more open than usual.

Doctor Paul Joseph Goebbels said recently that the nightly air raids have had a terrific effect upon the morale of the people of London. The good doctor is absolutely right. Today the morale of the people is higher than ever before. They are fused together not by fear but a surging spirit of courage the like of which the world has never known.

London Can Take It, *a short film produced by the British government,* 1940

1939–1945, LONDON EVACUEES

Once the inevitability of war was established, the government prepared to move vulnerable people, especially children, away from the city to the safety of the countryside, in a plan known as Operation Pied Piper. Evacuation was voluntary, but the government had launched an extensive public information campaign encouraging Londoners to leave the city.

Children often went to strangers, who were assessed on the quality of accommodation they could offer rather than on their suitability as host families.

PLATFORM 6

During the war I was sent to Devon, in the countryside. It was very scary being separated from my mother and father—didn't feel right to be away from them—but after a while I got used to it. I wrote my parents and uncles lots of letters and they wrote back.

Staying with a new family was very strange at first but they were very patient and welcoming. I still remember the first meal I ate with them. I didn't eat much, because I was so scared and upset, but the next night we had a meat pie with home-grown roast potatoes and vegetables, and I thought it was the best dinner I'd ever had.

Dorothy West, in Voices from the Second World War, *2016*

1945, VE DAY

After six years of fighting, Germany finally surrendered, and the war in Europe was over. British prime minister Winston Churchill declared May 8, 1945, an official day of "rejoicing" called Victory in Europe Day.

Londoners flooded the streets and more than a million people celebrated together. Churchill was reassured by the Ministry of Food that there were enough beer supplies in the capital.

This is VE DAY at last. . . . At midnight I insisted on our joining the revels. It was a very warm night. Thousands of searchlights swept the sky. Otherwise there were no illuminations and no street lights at all. Claridge's and the Ritz were lit up. We walked down Bond Street passing small groups singing, not boisterously. Piccadilly however was full of swarming people and littered with paper.

We walked arm in arm into the middle of Piccadilly Circus which was brilliantly illuminated with arc lamps. Here the crowds were yelling, singing and laughing.

James Lees-Milne, Prophesying Peace: Diaries 1944–1945, 1977

1948, THE LONDON OLYMPICS

Seven thousand pigeons were released at the opening ceremony of the 1948 Olympic Games in London, called the Austerity Games because of the difficult post-war economic climate. Rationing was still in effect in Britain, but athletes were given an increased allowance of 5,476 calories per day, the same amount allocated to dockworkers and miners, instead of the normal 2,600.

After years of austerity it's like a mighty audience brought up on gloomy black and white films and suddenly seeing their first "talkie"—and finding it's in colour, too. Imagine an emerald cut into an oblong and surrounded by a circlet of rust. That's the Wembley turf, enclosed by the track. Imagine a giant's sugar bowl full of coloured hundreds-and-thousands. That's what the stands look like when they are full.

Peter Wilson, The Sunday Mirror, *August 7, 1948*

1948, WINDRUSH

Between 1948 and 1971, half a million citizens from the Commonwealth settled in Britain.
Among the first to arrive were over eight hundred Caribbean residents who arrived on board
the *Empire Windrush*. The ship docked at Tilbury before passengers traveled on to London.
Many found a hostile and difficult reception as they came to live as British citizens.

Behind you
Windrush child
palm trees wave goodbye

above you
Windrush child
seabirds asking why

around you
Windrush child
blue water rolling by

beside you
Windrush child
your Windrush mum and dad

think of storytime yard
and mango mornings

and new beginnings
doors closing and opening

will things turn out right?
At least the ship will arrive
in midsummer light

and you Windrush child
think of Grandmother
telling you don't forget to write

and with one last hug
walk good walk good
and the sea's wheel carries on spinning

and from that place England
you tell her in a letter
of your Windrush adventure

stepping in a big ship
not knowing how long the journey
or that you're stepping into history

bringing your Caribbean eye
to another horizon
Grandmother's words your shining beacon

learning how to fly
the kite of your dreams
in an English sky

Windrush child
walking good walking good
in a mind-opening
meeting of snow and sun

John Agard, "Windrush Child,"
Under the Moon & Over the Sea, *2002*

1950s, A MULTICULTURAL CITY

By the last years of the twentieth century, London was becoming a multicultural and diverse city.

Marvel again at the market stalls
singing the earth's abundance
in the heaped-up homegrown freshness
of their own vernacular favoured names.

Not Aubergine but Balanjay
     Not Spinach but Calaloo
Not Green-beans but Bora
     Not Chilli but Bird-pepper
And not just any mango
     but the one crowned, Buxton Spice,

Still hiding its ambrosia in the roof
of my mouth, still flowering
like the bird-picked mornings
on the branches of my memory.

Grace Nichols, "Bourda,"
Passport to Here and There, *2020*

1950s, TOWER BLOCKS

There was a great need for functional and affordable housing after World War II, and in response modern tower blocks were built using concrete. These streets-in-the-sky added a new look to London's skyline. They are both celebrated and despised.

But where can be the heart that sends a family to the twentieth floor of such a slab as this?

John Betjeman, in Bird's Eye View, The Englishman's Home, *1969*

1952,
THE GREAT SMOG

The heavy yellow fogs of the Great Smog
were caused by air pollution. Also known as
"pea-soupers," they were so dense that people
struggled to see their own feet.

1966, THE NOTTING HILL CARNIVAL

In 1958, Caribbean residents of the Notting Hill area of London were the targets of racially motivated violence and property destruction. As part of the residents' response, they established an annual carnival to celebrate Caribbean culture. The outdoor version of the event began in 1966.

On days like these we dance to us,
With the drum beat of liberation
Under the close cover of European skies,
We dance like true survivors
We dance to the sounds of our dreams.
In the mirror we see
Rainbow people on the beat,
Everyday carnival folk like we.

Benjamin Zephaniah, "Carnival Days,"
Too Black, Too Strong, *2001*

1966, THE WEMBLEY WORLD CUP

On July 30, 1966, when England beat West Germany at Wembley Stadium, winning the FIFA World Cup final for the first time, there were celebrations all over London. People sang and danced in the streets and brought traffic in the West End to a complete stop.

"Its [*sic*] like VE night, election night and New Years [*sic*] Eve all rolled into one."

An Athletic Association spokesman, in The Observer, *July 31, 1966*

2022, THE DEATH OF QUEEN ELIZABETH II

When Queen Elizabeth II, the longest-reigning British monarch, died at the age of ninety-six, her coffin lay in state in Westminster Hall for four full days. An estimated 250,000 people lined up, in some cases for up to twenty-four hours, to pay their respects.

Evening will come, however determined the late afternoon,
Limes and oaks in their last green flush, pearled in September mist.
I have conjured a lily to light these hours, a token of thanks,
Zones and auras of soft glare framing the brilliant globes.
A promise made and kept for life – that was your gift –
Because of which, here is a gift in return, glovewort to some,
Each shining bonnet guarded by stern lance-like leaves.
The country loaded its whole self into your slender hands,
Hands that can rest, now, relieved of a century's weight.

Simon Armitage, "Floral Tribute,"
Tribute: Three Commemorative Poems, *2022*

EXTRA NOTES

1066, THE NORMANS: WILLIAM CROWNED KING

Shortly after his coronation, William the Conqueror sent a charter, now called the William Charter, to the city of London. William understood the importance of safeguarding London's wealth by ensuring the city's peaceful surrender. The William Charter confirmed the rights of London's citizens, particularly rights involving the succession of property, and won their support. Significantly, the charter is written in Old English instead of William's native Norman French.

c. 1100, STREET NAMES OF LONDON

Streets could even be named after fashions of the time period. For example, Piccadilly Circus gets its name from the trade of Robert Baker, a tailor living there who was famous for selling piccadills, wide lace collars that were fashionable in the late sixteenth century. Pudding Lane gets its name not from the dessert but the butchers of Eastcheap Market, who used the lane to transport offal, also known as pudding.

1215, MAGNA CARTA AND THE FIRST PARLIAMENT

London is the only city to be named in Magna Carta, and the document legitimized London's custom of appointing a mayor, who would work with the barons to ensure that the document's mandates were carried out. The role, now known as Lord Mayor of the City of London, still exists today.

1235, HENRY III STARTS A ROYAL MENAGERIE

Unfortunately, many of the animals did not fare well in London and their keepers were ill-equipped to look after them. An elephant was reportedly given wine in winter as it was believed the wine would keep it warm. It died a few years later, as did many other animals in these cold, cramped conditions.

Some historical sources claim that, under Elizabeth I, the public was allowed to see the menagerie for free, provided that they brought a dog or cat with them to feed the lions. The Tower menagerie could also prove dangerous to humans. A visitor was mauled and died shortly after she attempted to pat a lion, despite warnings not to get close to the animals.

1559, ELIZABETH I

Under Mary's reign, Elizabeth I had been imprisoned in the Tower of London and held under house arrest at Hampton Court. Years later, Elizabeth would return to the Tower of London on the eve of her coronation, with a jubilant crowd cheering her arrival. Her procession and coronation were carefully devised to distance Elizabeth from her mother's reputation as the traitor-queen.

1599, THE GLOBE THEATRE

Audiences came from all sectors of society, from criminals to the nobility, though they usually congregated separately.

Actors had often been treated with suspicion and disdain—viewed as unruly characters who offered a superfluous form of entertainment that was responsible for distracting young men from their work as well as keeping people away from church. Despite this reputation, the theater grew in popularity during the Elizabethan era.

1606, FIREWORKS NIGHT

The failure of the Gunpowder Plot was commemorated for two centuries with a state holiday, which was eventually suspended due to its association with anti-Catholic sentiments. The event is still remembered on Bonfire Night celebrations, when fireworks are let off, bonfires are lit, and "Guys"— effigies of Guy Fawkes—are burned.

1660, CHARLES II AND THE RESTORATION

In order to reassure Parliament that his return to England and restoration to the throne would be largely peaceful, Charles II issued the Declaration of Breda, offering a general pardon to anyone who sided with Parliament during the Civil War. However, this mercy did not extend to the men directly involved in his father's death.

Charles II's restoration brought other changes to England, as entertainments that had been restricted under Cromwell flourished again, including the theater. Charles supported the development of theaters and allowed women to appear onstage for the first time.

1675, THE GREENWICH OBSERVATORY

The purpose of the Royal Observatory was to reduce shipwrecks by solving the "longitude problem." Seafaring was key to Britain's trade ambitions, and while sailors were able to measure latitude quite accurately, the difficulty of correctly assessing longitude led to many lives being lost at sea.

Astronomers thought producing an accurate map of the stars would solve the navigational problem. Charles II appointed John Flamsteed as the first Astronomer Royal. Flamsteed lived in the Royal Observatory and was given an allowance of £100 per year.

1683–1684, FROST FAIR

Winters in Britain were particularly harsh between the fourteenth century and the mid-nineteenth century, a period known as the "Little Ice Age"—conditions were so extreme that they led to famine and loss of life. However, Londoners also saw them as an opportunity for enjoyment.

The magnificent fairs held on the frozen Thames included games, food stalls, pubs, and even an ice-skating rink. Sailors, now out of work due to the Thames freezing, would fit runners to small boats and offer rides across the ice. There were fox and rabbit hunts, and an elephant was paraded across the river during the last frost fair of 1814.

1703, BUCKINGHAM PALACE

After Buckingham Palace was bombed during World War II, Queen Elizabeth (mother of Queen Elizabeth II) is reported to have said, "I am glad we have been bombed. Now we can look the East End in the eye."

1738, GIN

Increasing rates of alcoholism led to a rise in London's social problems. Parliament passed a series of acts to restrict the gin trade. This was met with outrage from Londoners, and mobs formed, shouting, "No gin, no king!" However, the government persisted with new, stricter Gin Acts and by 1757 the Gin Craze had ended.

1794, DANDIES

Brummell reacted against the ostentatious male fashions popular in the eighteenth century, which included silk and satin garments in a rainbow of colors, perfumes, makeup, and powdered wigs. Instead, Brummell's style encapsulated the modern phrase "less is more" and emphasized elegance in the quality and fit of the clothes to flatter the masculine physique. His idea that a well-cut blue coat was suitable for all occasions was soon emulated all over London.

He also had revolutionary ideas in terms of personal hygiene and was considered eccentric for bathing in hot water every day, something even the rich didn't do in this time period. Other ideas were more extreme by modern standards such as shining his shoes with champagne. Brummell claimed he needed five hours to get dressed.

1850, VICTORIAN STREET LIFE

Mayhew was meticulous in his research into the great social problems of the time: he interviewed a huge variety of people, including mudlarks, who searched the mud along the river Thames for items to sell, and "pure finders," who collected dog feces to sell to tanners.

Mayhew's detailed notes included descriptions of people's living conditions, clothing, and habits, as well as calculated estimates of their income. By publishing these interviews, he gave voice to poor Londoners and provided insight into their struggles for his readers.

1851, THE GREAT EXHIBITION

The main venue for the Great Exhibition was the specially built Crystal Palace, a magnificent giant building of glass and iron, covering 18 acres. The event was open from May 1 to October 15, 1851, during which time it hosted over 15,000 contributors and six million visitors.

Initially an entry fee of £3 for gentlemen and £2 for ladies was charged, but this was eventually reduced to 1 shilling per person. Exhibits included printing presses, early bicycles, textile machines, and precious fabrics and jewels. One of the key features of interest was the public toilets, the first paid-for public flushing toilets in the UK. Intrigued visitors paid one penny to use these facilities.

1855, TRANSPORT

The omnibus, introduced to London by George Shillibeer, and the lighter cabriolet were both horse-drawn vehicles brought over from Paris that changed London's streets. The cabriolet typically seated two people, with a driver standing on a raised platform at the back, and is the origin of the English word *cab*.

Shillibeer's omnibus service resembled modern public transport as the omnibuses ran to a timetable and could be hailed along the route. They were drawn by a team of three horses, could carry twenty-two passengers, and became popular with middle-class commuters.

However, they did create a problem: large amounts of horse droppings. These were cleaned up by crossing sweepers for very little pay.

1860s, A MAP OF VICTORIAN LONDON

The effects of industrialization were especially apparent during the Victorian era as people experienced huge changes in the ways they lived and worked. It was a time characterized by groundbreaking new inventions and discoveries, and cramped, dirty housing and dangerous working conditions for the poor.

The map of the city featured several exciting new additions as many of London's iconic buildings were constructed during the Victorian era, including the Palace of Westminster, the Royal Albert Hall, the Victoria and Albert Museum, the Science Museum, and Saint Pancras railway station.

1908, DOUBLE-DECKER BUS

Initially, London buses were run by different operators and came in a variety of colors, denoting different routes, like modern London subway lines. In 1905, the London Motor Omnibus Company painted most of their vehicles red, which eventually became the iconic color still used for buses today.

1914, WORLD WAR I

Lord Herbert Kitchener, the secretary of state for war,, was the face of the recruitment campaign to increase the size of Britain's army. Many recruitment drives were held at Trafalgar Square and were helped by a series of persuasive enlistment posters and patriotic music played on gramophones. White feathers were sometimes handed to men not in uniform as a symbol of cowardice.

By December 1915, the number of volunteers to have joined the British Army had reached 2,446,719, but as the number of men enlisting dwindled and casualties mounted, the government passed the Military Service Act and introduced conscription. Conscription was unpopular and over 200,000 people demonstrated against it in Trafalgar Square in April 1916.

1939, WORLD WAR II

Shortly after Neville Chamberlain's announcement, air raid sirens sounded. Londoners rushed to the nearest shelters, although some at the British Broadcasting Company (BBC) put on tin helmets and went to the building's roof to watch the bombs fall. However, there was nothing to see as it turned out to be a false alarm.

1940–1941, THE BLITZ

The Blitz was a German campaign to destroy the British economy, weaken morale, and force Britain out of the war. The plan failed and Britain's victory in the Battle of Britain contributed to the eventual destruction of the Third Reich. The term "Blitz spirit" was coined to demonstrate British stoicism and determination in the face of death and destruction. However, historians have argued that this idea of heroic national unity has been exaggerated and in reality, many Londoners were demoralized by the ruins of their city and haunted by the deaths of so many.

In order to protect themselves from German bombs, many Londoners sought shelter in subway stations. Despite initial reluctance, the government changed its policy and commissioned London Transport to build deep-level shelters. It is estimated that up to 170,000 people took shelter in underground stations during World War II.

Many of London's iconic buildings, including Buckingham Palace, the Tower of London, and the Houses of Parliament, were badly damaged. Some areas were so thoroughly destroyed that they had to be entirely rebuilt after the war.

WE ARE GRATEFUL TO THE FOLLOWING FOR PERMISSION TO REPRODUCE COPYRIGHTED MATERIAL:

"The Great Fire of London" by George Szirtes, from *In the Land of the Giants*, Salt Publishing, 2012,
"The Great Fire of London" © George Szirtes, 2012, reproduced by kind permission of the author.

"Sir Christopher Wren" by Edmund Clerihew Bentley, reproduced with permission of Curtis Brown Group Ltd.,
London, on behalf of the Estate of E. Clerihew Bentley. Copyright © E. Clerihew Bentley 1905.

Winter Notes on Summer Impressions by Fyodor Dostoevsky, Alma Books, 1863,
translated by Kyril Zinovieff, reproduced by permission of Alma Books.

"The First Escalator" from *The Londoner's Almanac* by Russell Ash, copyright © Russell Ash, 1985, permission sought.

The text on p. 176 is quoted in *Testament of Youth*, by Vera Brittain.
Texts by Vera Brittain are © The Literary Executors of the Vera Brittain Will Trust [1970].

Dorothy West in *Voices from the Second World War*, Walker Books, published in association with *First News*
and the Silver Line, 2016; excerpt copyright © Dorothy West, 2016, reproduced by permission of *First News*.

Prophesying Peace: Diaries 1944–1945 by James Lees-Milne, John Murray,
reproduced by permission of David Higham Associates.

"Windrush Child" by John Agard, from *Under the Moon & Over the Sea*, Walker Books, 2001,
copyright © John Agard, 2001, reproduced by kind permission of John Agard c/o Caroline Sheldon Literary Agency Ltd.

"Bourda" by Grace Nichols, from *Passport to Here and There*, Bloodaxe Books, 2020, copyright © Grace Nichols, 2020,
reproduced with permissions from Curtis Brown Group Ltd. on behalf of Grace Nichols.

"Carnival Days" by Benjamin Zephaniah, from *Too Black, Too Strong*, Bloodaxe Books, 2001,
copyright © Benjamin Zephaniah, 2001, reproduced with permission of Bloodaxe Books.

Excerpt from "London Goes Wild for Cup Victors," *The Observer*, Sunday, July 31, 1966,
courtesy of Guardian News & Media Ltd.

"Floral Tribute" by Simon Armitage from *Tribute: Three Commemorative Poems*, Faber and Faber Ltd., 2022,
"Floral Tribute" copyright © Simon Armitage, 2022, reproduced by permission of Faber and Faber Ltd.
and David Godwin Associates.

EVERY REASONABLE EFFORT HAS BEEN MADE TO TRACE OWNERSHIP OF AND/OR SECURE PERMISSION
FOR THE USE OF COPYRIGHTED MATERIAL. IF NOTIFIED OF ANY ERROR OR OMISSION, THE
PUBLISHER WILL GLADLY MAKE ANY NECESSARY CORRECTIONS IN FUTURE REPRINTS.

Copyright © 2024 by Laura Carlin • All rights reserved. No part of this book may be reproduced, transmitted, or stored in an information retrieval system in any form or by any means, graphic, electronic, or mechanical, including photocopying, taping, and recording, without prior written permission from the publisher. • First US edition 2024 • First published by Walker Books Ltd. (UK) 2024 • Library of Congress Catalog Card Number pending • ISBN 978-1-5362-3143-4 • This book was typeset in Historical Fell Type and WB Laura Carlin. • The illustrations were done in watercolor, ink, oil pastel, and colored pencil. Candlewick Studio, an imprint of Candlewick Press, 99 Dover Street, Somerville, Massachusetts 02144 • www.candlewickstudio.com Printed in Humen, Dongguan, China • 24 25 26 27 28 29 APS 10 9 8 7 6 5 4 3 2 1

For Claudia and John

The Museum of London was a huge inspiration for this book.
May it always be such an inspiration and open to everyone.

Thank you to Walker Books, especially Denise, Ben,
Meera, and Marina, for embarking on this adventure
and for managing to stay so enthusiastic and
patient throughout. Thank you to Mel, Jesse, and
Joanna, and to my family for sticking with me.